S0-BAL-414

I
Know
A
Giraffe

I Know A

Giraffe

A Tall Tale by

DAVID OMAR WHITE

J. EUGENE SMITH LIBRARY
EASTERN CONN. STATE UNIVERSITY
WILLIMANTIC, CT 06226-2295

ESEA TITLE II
REGIONAL READING PROJECT
EASTERN CONN. STATE COLLEGE
LIBRARY

Alfred A. Knopf : New York

L. C. Catalog card number: 63-14609

This is a Borzoi Book, published by Alfred A. Knopf, Inc.

Copyright ©1965 by David Omar White.
All rights reserved. No part of this book may be reproduced
in any form without permission in writing from the publisher,
except by a reviewer, who may quote brief passages and
reproduce not more than three illustrations in a review to be
printed in a magazine or newspaper. Manufactured in the United
States of America, and distributed by Random House, Inc.
Published simultaneously in Toronto, Canada,
by Random House of Canada, Limited.

For Nat and Amy

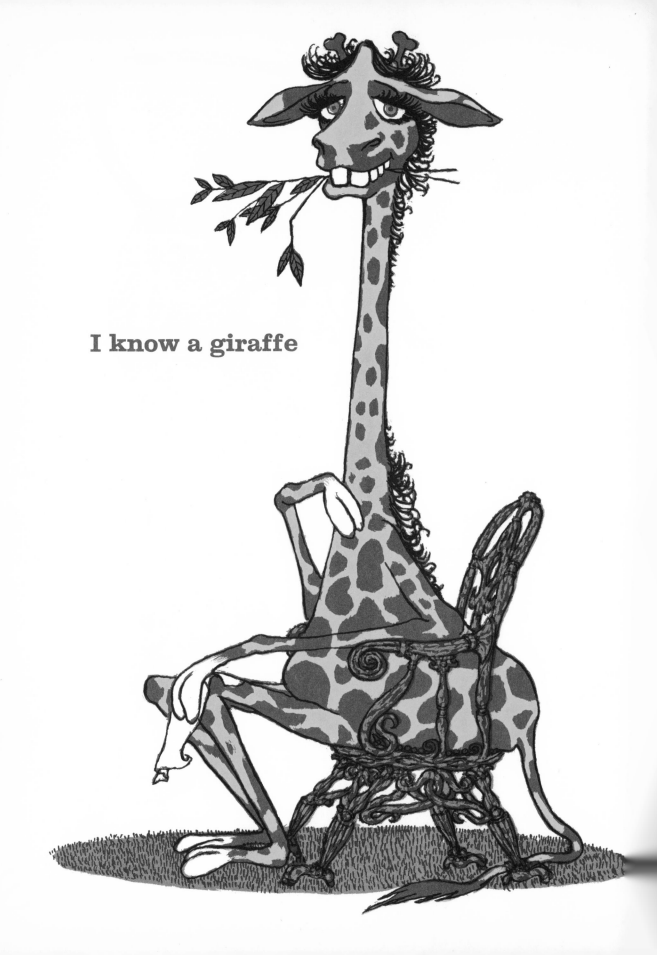

I know a giraffe

with no neck at all

and his hair grows over his eyes.

He's really only one foot tall.

(He's awfully small for his size.)

He lives with my aunt

and eats her pies

and he's getting to be terribly FAT!

He may be no giraffe at all.

He might be a . . .

PERSIAN CAT!

I know a cat

who is much too fat

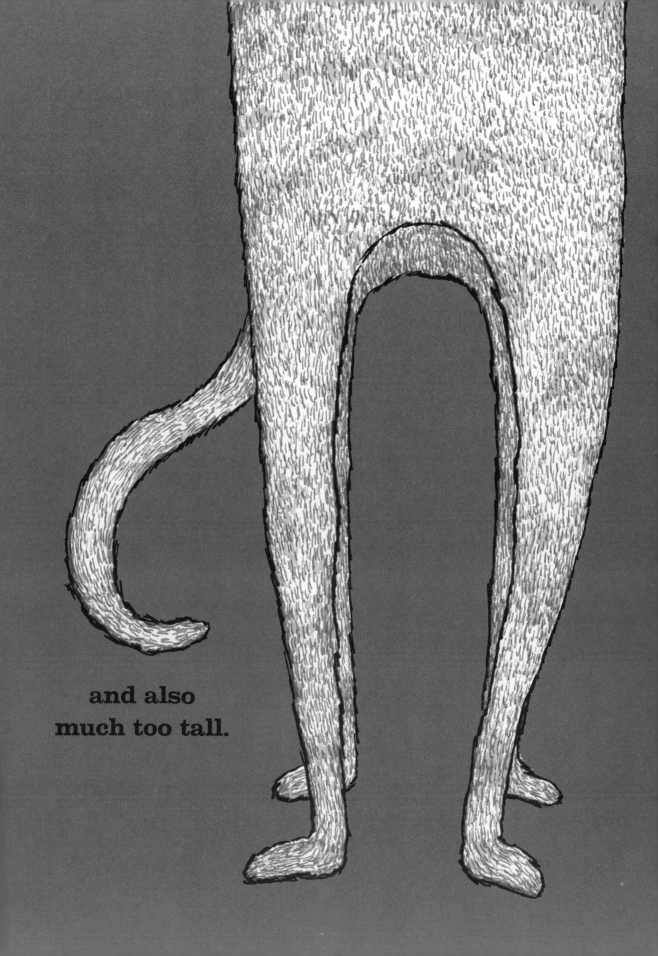

and also
much too tall.

He's too fat for the sofa

and

too

tall

for

the

hall.

In fact, he won't fit in the house at all.

He eats milk and cream
and wild gooseberries

and hot dogs

and spareribs

and

maraschino cherries

and sauerkraut

and, most of all,

HONEY.

And he does something else
                I think is quite funny—
he'll dance for his supper
at a circus or fair,

which is rare
for a cat
but not for a . . .

BEAR!

I know a bear
who is ever so pretty

and runs willy nilly
all over the city.

Not only Willy, but other folks, too,
can ride all around for a nickel or two.

He's the unusualest bear
I ever have seen,
he's pawless
and clawless
and yellow
and green.

And when blocked by the traffic,
he causes a scene.

I think that perhaps the joke is on us.
It could be he's only a . . .

HOBOKEN BUS!

I know a bus that runs on my street
on four skinny legs, on four funny feet.

There isn't any room for people inside,

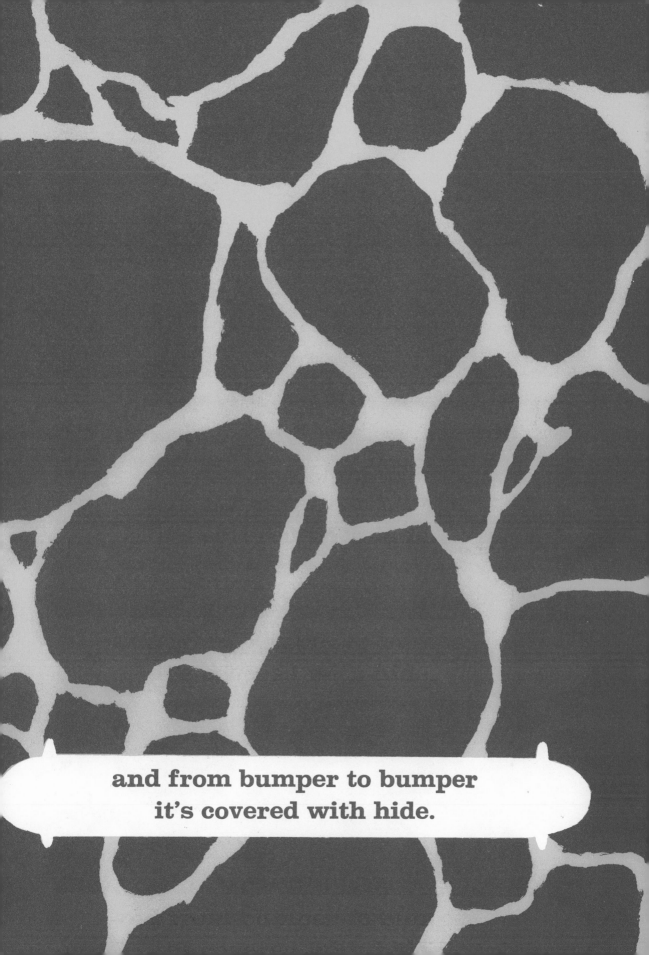

**and from bumper to bumper
it's covered with hide.**

It has a long neck
where the driver should be.

HA HA. HO HO.

(And also HEE HEE.)

I know a giraffe

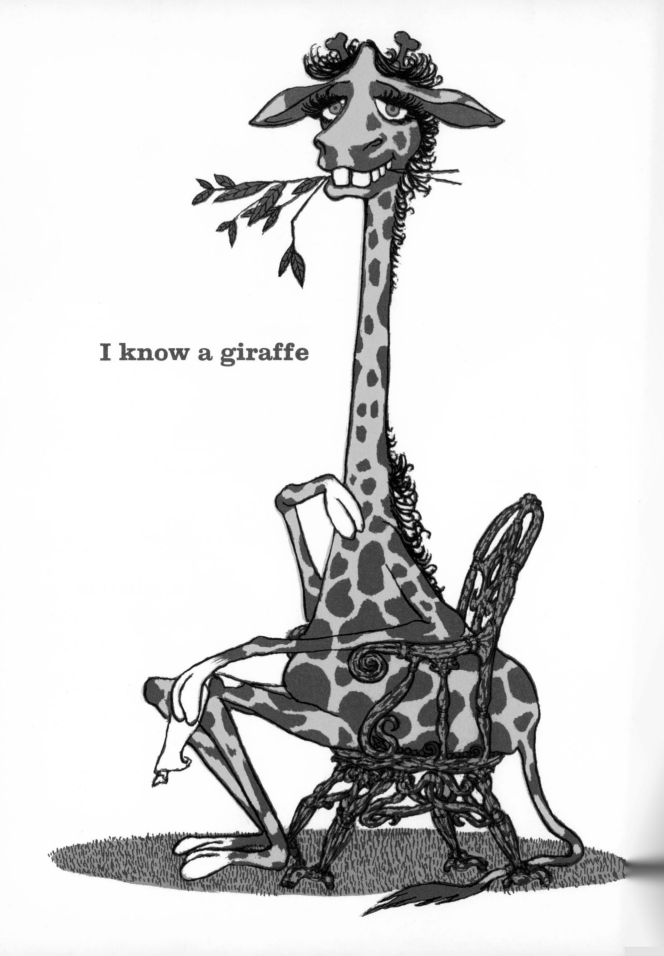

and a giraffe

knows

ME!